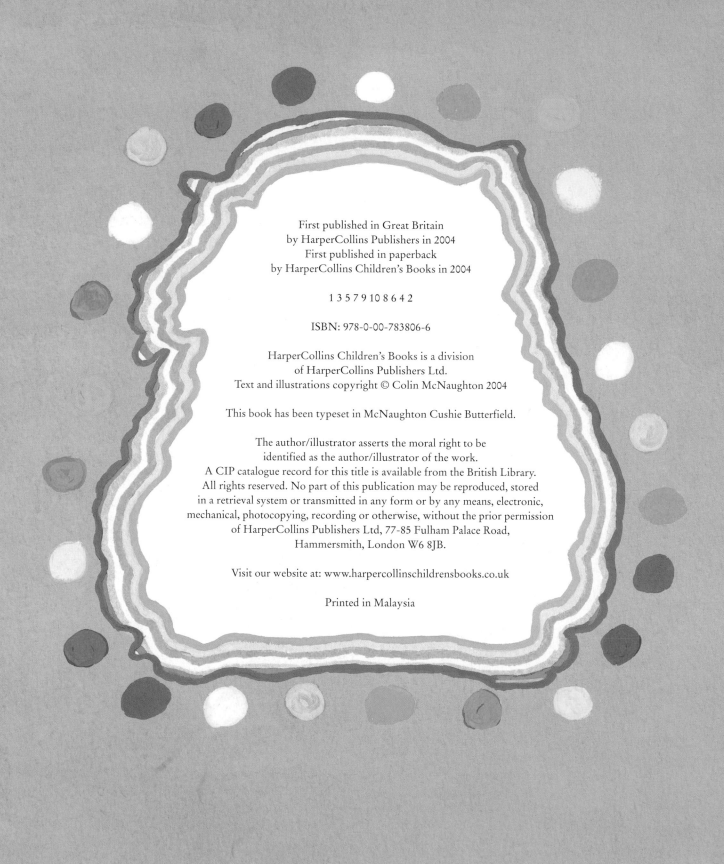

First published in Great Britain
by HarperCollins Publishers in 2004
First published in paperback
by HarperCollins Children's Books in 2004

1 3 5 7 9 10 8 6 4 2

ISBN: 978-0-00-783806-6

HarperCollins Children's Books is a division
of HarperCollins Publishers Ltd.
Text and illustrations copyright © Colin McNaughton 2004

This book has been typeset in McNaughton Cushie Butterfield.

Visit our website at: www.harpercollinschildrensbooks.co.uk

Printed in Malaysia

Colin McNaughton

Cushie Butterfield

(She's a Little Cow)

HarperCollins *Children's Books*

'I'm not well,' said
Cushie Butterfield
on Monday morning
(a school day).

'Sick!'
said her mummy.

'I'm under the weather,' said Cushie Butterfield on Tuesday morning (a school day).

'Sick!'
said her dad.

'I've got the collywobbles,'
said Cushie Butterfield
on Wednesday morning
(a school day).

'Sick!'

said Sam Samson, who's the next-door neighbours' lad.

'I'm sick as a parrot!'
said Cushie Butterfield
on Thursday morning
(a school day).

'Sick!'
said the doctor.

'I've taken a turn for the worse,'
said Cushie Butterfield
on Friday morning
(a school day).

'Sick!'

said the nurse.

'All better!' said Cushie Butterfield on Saturday morning (not a school day) and she went out to play.

'Strange!'

said the lady with
the alligator purse.

'I'm as fit as a fiddle!' said Cushie Butterfield on Sunday morning (not a school day) and she played all day.

'Odd!'

said Uncle Billy.

'Sick!'

said Cushie Butterfield on Monday morning (a school day).

'Weird!'
said Auntie Jean.

'Bizarre!'
said Nana Dixie on the telephone machine.

That night, when Cushie
Butterfield was asleep,
her mum decided to
clean under her bed.

This is what she found...

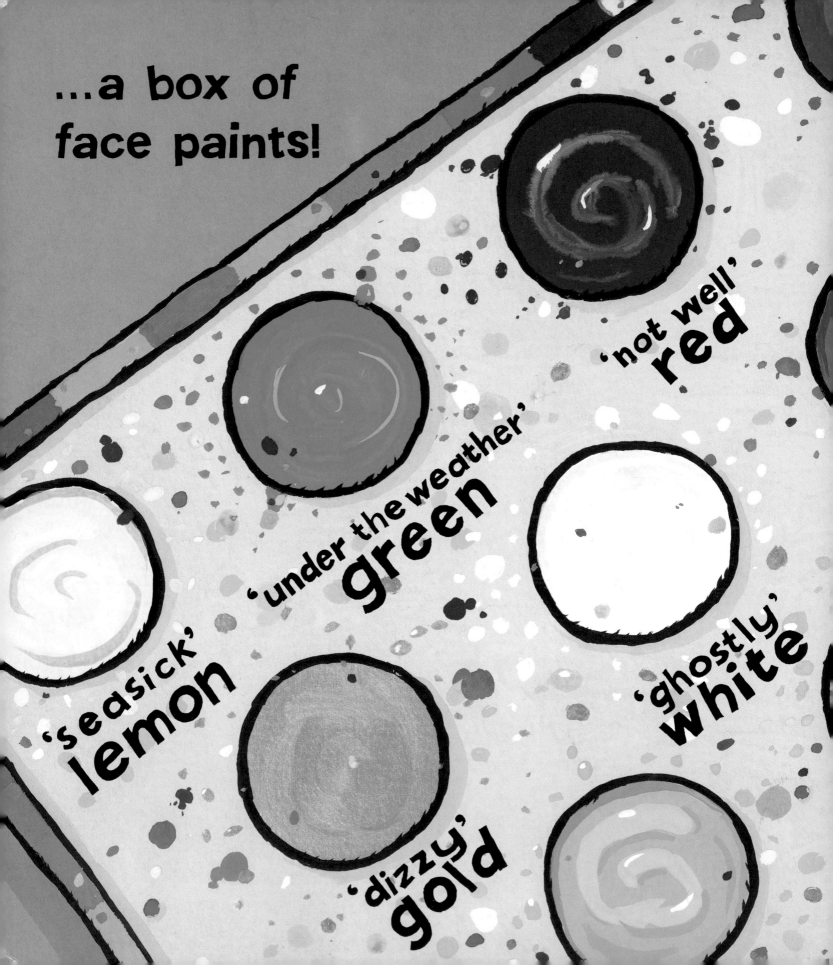

On Tuesday morning Cushie Butterfield went to school.